Roland

by Nelly Stéphane

pictures by André François

ENCHANTED LION BOOKS

NEW YORK

Roland was late to school.

"Stand in the corner," said the teacher, which Roland did.

But there was nothing to do in the corner, so with his pencil Roland drew a long tiger on the wall. Then he said: "CRACK!" and the tiger came to life.

The tiger stretched himself out to his full length and very politely said good morning to the teacher.

"We've no room for you here," said the teacher, and he opened the door. Without another word the tiger went away.

"Everybody out for recess now," said the teacher. "As for you, Roland, you stay in. See to it that you don't say 'CRACK' again."

Roland was alone in the classroom with nothing to do. He drew a zebra in his notebook, tore out the page, and stuck it on the window.

The other boys were throwing snowballs in the yard. A snowball smashed into the window. The breaking glass went "CRACK" and the zebra came to life. Down into the yard it jumped and over the wall.

The teacher had not seen a thing because another snowball had hit him in the eye. Not very hard, luckily.

After recess, lessons began again. The wind was blowing hard outside. Snow came flying in through the broken window and filled the room.

Roland forgot what the teacher had said. He drew twenty fir-trees, three brown bears, two chestnut bears, and a stream and said: "CRACK! CRACK! CRACK! CRACK!" The stream flowed and the bears walked in the snow!

Then the teacher told all the children to go home because the classroom had grown too cold.

In the street Roland met his friend Isabel. She was wearing her fur coat. Roland patted the coat and said: "CRACK!" The coat came to life and turned into many little fur animals. People tried to catch them, but the fur animals ran away.

"You've stolen my coat," cried Isabel.
So the police took Roland to prison.

One of the little fur animals went in search of Roland. This one knew how to open doors. With its help, Roland escaped while the guard was sleeping.

Roland and the fur animal walked across roof after roof.

Then the fur animal took Roland down a chimney. They were going to visit a poor little girl who had no toys.

Roland drew a large doll on the floor and said: "Crack!"

At once the doll came to life and began to dance. They all clapped their hands and sang.

But soon it was time for Roland to go home. The dancing doll said she wanted to stay with the little girl and play with her.

The fur animal wanted to go back to his brothers. They all said good-bye.

Roland and the fur animal went down to the street, shook hands, and went their separate ways.

In the middle of a large square two ladies were arguing over a cab pulled by a zebra.

It was Roland's zebra.

Roland made a signal with his hand.

The zebra freed itself and came to him, leaving the ladies still arguing.

Roland climbed up on the zebra's back and off they galloped.

The zebra bounded down a hilly street. A banana skin was lying in the gutter and . . .

The zebra slipped on it and fell!

Roland shot into the air and went headfirst into a canal, but he didn't hurt himself a bit.

Swimming in the canal, he caught a swordfish. Then he saw a wonderful, shining fish behind it. He let the swordfish go and swam after the shining fish.

The shining fish was flat. Roland put it in his pocket and climbed out of the water to go home.

He felt sad because he had lost his zebra. To cheer himself up, he drew two donkeys on the ground and said: "CRACK!" so the donkeys came to life and went home with Roland.

When they got there, his mother gave him a big jug for the shining fish. But it had stopped shining. Roland put it back in his pocket.

He told his mother why he was late for lunch.

Then his mother said at once: "You must go and tell Isabel you're sorry that you made her coat run away."

Isabel was in bed. She had caught a cold without her coat.

But she was ashamed of herself for having put Roland in prison, so she was glad to see him again.

Roland gave her the fish as a present.

And at once it began to shine.

When Roland got home, he found not only the two donkeys but the zebra as well. It had come back while he was away.

"Keep the two donkeys and the zebra," his mother said. "But you must promise not to say 'CRACK' ever again. Our apartment is not big enough for any more animals."

Roland felt a little sad, but he had his homework to do–and it was not so bad after all with his animals beside him.

Only the cat was annoyed. He had wanted to eat the shining fish!

End